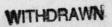

Also by Jill Tomlinson

Jill Tomlinson

The Aardvark
Who Wasn't Sure

Illustrated by Susan Hellard

195827

First published in Great Britain 1973
by Methuen Children's Books Ltd
Magnet paperback edition published 1980
Reissued 1989 by Mammoth
This edition published 1991 by Mammoth
an imprint of Egmont Children's Books Limited
Michelin House, 81 Fulham Road, London SW3 6RB

Reprinted 1991, 1992 (twice), 1994 (twice), 1995 (twice),
1996 (twice), 1997 (twice), 1998 (twice)

Text copyright © 1973 The Estate of Jill Tomlinson
Illustrations copyright © 1991 Susan Hellard

ISBN 0 7497 0863 8

A CIP catalogue record for this title
is available from the British Library

Printed and bound in Great Britain
by Cox & Wyman Ltd, Reading, Berkshire

Contents

For DL and his children
Claire, Annushska and Tamara,
not forgetting
the D that I never leave out, DH

1 · 'What's termites?'

Pim was an aardvark.

His mother said so.

But Pim was a very new aardvark and he was not at all sure *what* he was.

At first he didn't care very much. He lived in his cosy dark burrow and his mother fed him warm milk when he was hungry. Between his feeds he just slept, like most babies.

But as he grew bigger, he began to notice things. One day he woke up to find that his mother wasn't there. He had thought that she was always with him. He shuffled around the burrow looking for her but he couldn't find her. Then he found a sort of sloping tunnel.

Perhaps she was up there. He began to shuffle along it. Then he heard scraping sounds. Something was coming down the tunnel towards him! He backed into the burrow just in time. His mother burst in, nearly knocking him over.

'Pim!' she said. 'You're supposed to be asleep.'

'You were supposed to be here!' shouted Pim, who had been rather frightened. 'Where have you been?'

'Where have I been? Getting food, of course. I have to eat sometimes.'

'Food?' said Pim.

'Termites,' his mother said. 'You have milk now, but when you're bigger you'll eat termites.'

'Why?' said Pim. 'Why will I eat termites?'

'Because you're an aardvark. Aardvarks eat termites. Now, do you want your feed or are you going to ask silly questions all night?'

Pim was hungry, so he had his feed. But as soon as his tummy felt full, he asked the

8

question that was bothering him.

'What's termites?'

'Go to sleep,' said his mother. 'You'll find out soon enough.'

'But what are they like?' Pim asked. 'I only want to know.'

'Oh dear,' said Pim's mother. 'I have a feeling you're the kind who never stops wanting to know.'

'Well?' said Pim. 'What's termites?'

'What *are* termites,' his mother corrected him. 'Crawly things. They are very like ants. They live in big nests that we have to rip open. They're nice, termites. Soft and juicy. You'll like them.'

'Rip open their nests?' said Pim. 'How?'

'With the claws on our front feet. We're very strong, you know.'

'How do I know I'm very strong?' said Pim doubtfully.

'Because you're an aardvark. Now go to sleep.'

Pim was very sleepy and dropped off almost

at once. That evening his mother had a surprise for him.

'Would you like to come with me tonight?' she asked him. 'I think it's time you saw the world outside.'

'Oh yes,' said Pim. 'Can I eat some termites?'

'Well, I don't think so,' his mother said. 'I shouldn't think you'd like them yet. But you can watch me so that you'll know what to do when you're big enough to get them yourself.'

So a little later Pim the aardvark followed his mother up the tunnel and stepped out just a little way into the African night. As far as he could see the land stretched out, flat and empty.

'The world is very big,' Pim said, moving closer to his mother.

'It is,' she said. 'Now, be very quiet and listen. We have to see if it's safe to go out.'

Pim's mother stood very still and pricked up her long ears

Pim copied her. At first he could hear nothing, but soon he became aware of a soft swishing noise all around them. He looked at his mother. It didn't seem to be bothering her.

'What's that?' he asked her. 'That whispering.'

'Just the grasses,' she said.

Suddenly there was a muffled roar—and then again.

'What's that?' said Pim, quivering all over.

'A lion,' she said. 'It's all right, it's a long way away. I don't think it will bother us. Now, let's see if you can run.'

Pim's mother began to move forward in a shambling gallop.

Pim didn't know how to begin. He stood transfixed for a second, unable to move.

Then he heard the lion roar again.

Pim found that he could run.

They travelled across the veldt for some way, Pim's mother lolloping gently so that Pim could keep up with her. Pim began to enjoy it. This was much more fun than staying at home in the earth burrow.

They passed a few scrubby trees. Then they came to some huge humps in the ground of all shapes and sizes. Pim's mother stopped suddenly, in front of the very biggest one.

'This will do,' she said. 'Now, watch.'

Pim watched as his mother began to tear at the side of the hump with her powerful claws. Soon she had made a gaping hole.

Then Pim saw a termite, and another and another. They came pouring out of the hole in panic. They didn't like having their nest broken open like this. Mrs Aardvark began to shoot out her long, sticky pink tongue and lick them up. Tongueful after tongueful of termites disappeared like magic. Then she pushed her long muzzle right into the nest, through the hole she had made, to lick up the rest of the termites.

Pim was amazed. Although the termites were tiny, they had very fierce faces and he wouldn't fancy putting *his* nose right inside one of their nests.

Still, if that's what aardvarks did, he would have to learn to do it. He put out his tongue and looked down at it. Yes, it was very long and pink and curly at the end, just like his mother's. When his mother turned round, her dinner finished, she found him sitting on his tail pulling faces. He was trying to shoot his tongue in and out, keeping his eyes on it all the time. This gave him a terrible squint.

'What are you doing?' laughed his mother.

'I am practising being an aardvark,' said Pim with dignity. He stopped and looked at his mother.

'Do you really like termites?' he said. 'They look horrible to me.'

'Delicious,' said his mother. 'That was a lovely dinner. But I expect you'd rather have some milk, wouldn't you? Come on then. Home.'

So Pim and his mother galloped home across the veldt.

2 · Monkey business

Pim was very tired after his first outing. He slept all day and all night.

When he woke up his mother was just coming back from her night's termite hunt. Pim was furious.

'You went without me!' he shouted. 'You left me behind.'

'Yes, dear,' said his mother. 'You were fast asleep and I thought it would be best if I left you.'

'I wanted to come. You should have waited for me.' Pim was very disappointed, which was why he was so cross.

'Aren't you hungry?' said his mother, who

14

understood. 'Come and have your feed. Then you can go up the tunnel and sit in the sun and watch the world go by for a little while if you like.'

This seemed a very nice idea. Pim *was* hungry, very hungry. He settled down for a good feed and soon felt much better.

'I'm sorry I was so cross,' he said, looking up at his mother, 'but it's so dull in this old hole.'

'This dull old hole is *safe*,' Mrs Aardvark said. 'Remember that. You may go up to the entrance now, but stay close to it. There's nothing like a dull old hole to dive into in time of danger.'

15

Pim set off up the tunnel.

When he came out at the top, he couldn't see at all at first. The sun was very bright and he sat down on his tail and blinked hard, his ears pricked up to listen for danger.

He wasn't sure what danger would sound like but the grunting sounds he heard didn't sound very dangerous. As his eyes became used to the sunlight, he saw that the grunts were coming from a band of animals which were moving around and pulling up grass-heads and other plants. They were stuffing these into their mouths with their forefeet, which were much more bendy than Pim's. He tried to pull up a plant with one of his front paws, but he couldn't get hold of it at all.

Oh well, if they ate plants, they probably didn't eat aardvarks. Pim settled down to doze in the sun.

Suddenly, a voice said 'Hello!' right by his ear.

Pim sat up quickly and backed towards his

16

burrow. He saw that one of the animals he had been watching had come up to him. He was quite small.

'Er . . . hello. What are you?' Pim asked him.

'I'm a baboon. A sort of monkey, my uncle says. What are you?'

'An aardvark.'

'An odd what?' The little baboon was staring at Pim as if he had never seen anything quite like him before.

'An *aardvark*,' said Pim clearly, 'a very new aardvark.'

'I'm a very new baboon,' said the funny

little animal, '*very* new. I don't know anything about anything yet.'

'Neither do I,' said Pim, who liked his new friend, 'except that my mother eats termites. Where do you live?'

'Where?' said the little baboon, puzzled. 'Well, everywhere. We move about all the time looking for food. At least, the grown-ups in the group do. I have milk from my mother. I like that.'

'So do I,' said Pim. 'But where do you sleep to be safe? Haven't you got a hole?'

'A hole?' said the baboon in surprise. 'No. We go up into some rocks or trees to rest.'

'Different ones every day?' said Pim. 'That must be interesting. I live in the same old hole all the time.' He nodded towards his burrow.

'Under the ground?' The baboon peered down it doubtfully. 'Haven't you ever been up a tree?'

'A tree?' Pim asked. 'I'm not sure. . . .'

'Those are trees, over there.' The little

baboon pointed to them. 'There's my uncle on top of that tall one. He's look-out today. Which reminds me—my mother will be looking out for me.'

Just at that moment, the baboon up the tree began to make a sharp barking noise, and all the other baboons began to rush about barking too.

'A lion!' squeaked Pim's new friend. 'Oh dear, I want my mother. Oh, here she is.' A big baboon rushed up to them. The baby scrambled on to her back and hung on to her fur. He rode her like a jockey rides a horse as she rushed back to join the troop. They all banded together in one big family—there were other babies on their mothers' backs as well as Pim's friend—and rushed off towards the trees, barking hard.

What a fuss! All Pim had to do was go down his tunnel.

He did so. His mother opened one eye.

'What's the matter?' she said.

'Lion,' said Pim. 'The baboons warned me.'

'Ah, you've learned about baboons. They are a help. When baboons bark, you dive for home or if you're too far away you dig a hole quickly.'

'Baboons climb trees. Why don't we climb trees?'

'We can't climb. What *are* you doing? You're scratching me.'

Pim was trying to pull himself up on to his mother's back, but he kept sliding down on to her tail.

'You're the wrong shape,' he complained. 'I wanted a ride like baboons have.'

'I'm not a baboon,' said Pim's mother. 'I am a tired aardvark. Now go to sleep if you want to come with me tonight.'

Pim did want to, so he curled himself up into a little ball to sleep.

But there was something else he wanted to ask: why don't we live in a big family with lots of others, instead of just by ourselves?

He knew the answer, though.

Because he was an aardvark.

Pim went to sleep.

3 · Big business

That night Mrs Aardvark took Pim with her on her feeding trip across the veldt. They went a different way this time. They passed through a belt of trees, or what had once been a belt of trees. Lots of them had been rooted up and thrown to the ground, and those that were still standing had their bark stripped off. There were broken branches every-where. Pim stopped and stared around him. What could have done this? Something *huge*.

'Elephants,' said his mother. 'Oh, they *are* messy eaters. Come on. We'll go round the edge.'

'Eaters?' said Pim, following his mother. 'Do they eat aardvarks?'

'No, just grass and branches and tree bark and things. But they will throw it around so. If they fancy a branch they can't reach, they just uproot the whole tree to get at it.'

'Elephants must be very strong,' said Pim, imagining a sort of giant baboon pulling up trees with its hands. 'I don't think I want to meet an elephant.'

The termite nest which his mother chose for her dinner was near a river. Pim watched his mother tearing at the nest for a while, but an interesting smell from the river drew him like a magnet.

Soon he was bumbling along by the river bank, snuffling busily. He had to watch out for tree roots which seemed to be spread out everywhere to trip him up. A tree loomed up ahead of him, and he stepped sideways to go round it.

That was funny. Pim stopped dead. The tree had moved!

Pim shook his head briskly. Trees didn't move. He looked over his shoulder.

There were four trees moving towards him. This was too much. Pim was going back to his mother. He was about to bolt when a voice above his head said, 'Hello.'

Something nuzzled his ear. Pim looked up. Two little eyes were looking at him down a long, long nose. Behind this face were two great ears and a huge body with . . . yes, the trees were the animal's legs!

'Er . . . hello,' Pim said warily. He was still ready to run. 'What are you?'

'I'm an elephant,' said the strange creature, 'a baby elephant.'

'A *baby* elephant?' said Pim, his eyes wide. 'Your mother must be enormous.'

'Well, she is quite big,' said the baby elephant. 'I stand underneath her for shade when the sun is hot. But what are you?'

'An aardvark,' said Pim.

'An odd what?' the elephant said. He

explored Pim all over with his trunk. 'You're certainly an odd something.'

'An *aardvark*,' Pim said. 'You can talk anyway. What a very odd dangly nose you've got. Stop tickling me.'

'Sorry,' said the elephant, withdrawing his trunk and holding it up. 'This is my trunk. I always use it for exploring odd . . . I mean, new things. It's very strong too. Watch.' He coiled his trunk around a small tree and yanked it right out of the ground, roots and all.

'So that's how you do it,' Pim said. 'I thought you must have hands, like baboons, for pulling things up with.' He looked at the tree on the ground. 'Aren't you going to eat it?'

'Eat it? No,' said the elephant, 'I still have milk from my mother.'

'Me too,' said Pim. He looked up at his strange new friend. 'Do elephants have holes?'

'Holes?' said the elephant. 'What would I need a hole for?'

'Well, to be safe in. Aren't you afraid of anything – lions and things?'

The baby elephant drew himself up very tall. 'The elephant is the king of the beasts. He is afraid of nothing,' he said proudly.

Then he grinned down at Pim. 'Or so my Auntie says. Actually, lions do attack baby elephants sometimes, and that's why I'm supposed to stay close to her or my mother.' He looked towards the river where there were splashing noises. 'I'd better get back to them –

they're crossing the river. Would you like to come and see me off?'

Pim said he would, and that's how he came to watch a herd of elephants at bath-time.

There seemed to be elephants everywhere, squirting themselves and each other with water and churning up the mud with their huge feet. Pim's friend could hardly wait to join them. With a cheery 'Bye-ee!' he slid down the slippery mudbank and landed in the water with a great splash. A huge elephant – it must have been his mother – sploshed up to him, spanked him with her trunk and then sprayed him all over with water. Pim's friend squealed and pretended to try and run away, but he was pulled back and squirted again and again. He was obviously enjoying himself hugely.

Pim was too as his mother saw when she found him a little later on. He was watching his friend being tugged up the steep bank on the other side of the river by his mother, while another elephant shoved him from behind. They were having quite a job getting him up the slippery slope. The king of the beasts *was* just a baby.

'So there you are,' Pim's mother said. 'Look at you. You're covered with mud. What have you been doing?'

'I got a bit splashed, that's all. Elephants are messy bathers as well as messy eaters. Oh look, they've got him up at last.'

His friend, who was tired after his difficult scramble, had grasped his mother's tail with his trunk. She pulled him after her into the scrub.

Pim sighed. He was tired too. He turned to his mother. She had a lovely big tail, bigger than Mrs Elephant's.

'Why haven't *I* got a trunk?' he said wistfully.

'Because you're an aardvark,' said his mother. 'Come on. Home.'

4 · A rotten digger

It was a long way home. Pim was very tired. He found it difficult to keep up with his mother, although she tried to go slowly.

At last he stopped altogether and she had to go back for him.

'Come on, Pim,' she said, 'it isn't far now.'

'My legs are squashing my feet!' he wailed. 'And my tail's heavy.'

'Oh dear,' she said, 'I forget how new you are. I know what we'll do. You needn't go any further. I'll make a new burrow right here. It seems a good place.'

While Pim blinked his tired eyes, she began to dig and dig and dig. In a few minutes the front half of her disappeared into the ground. Soon only her tail remained at the top and that was disappearing fast.

Was Pim going to be left all by himself? He was just going to tug at her tail to remind her that he was there when Mrs Aardvark backed out suddenly and nearly knocked him over.

'I hadn't forgotten you,' she said, seeing his face. 'Come on, sleepy, you'll be quite safe in here.' She began to push him into the hole she had made.

'Is this it?' said Pim. 'Is this the new burrow?' He didn't think much of it.

'No, of course it isn't. This is just a safe place where I can leave you while I'm busy digging. Now, tuck your tail in and I'll come and fetch you when our new home is ready.'

So Pim curled up snout to tail in the shallow hole and went to sleep. It was nearly light when his mother woke him up.

'Come on,' she said. 'Home.'

'I thought we weren't going home,' said Pim, stretching and coming out of his little hole.

30

'Not the old home, the new one,' his mother said. 'Here we are. It's right next door.'

There was an entrance tunnel and then a big roomy burrow beyond. In fact, it was exactly the same as their old home.

'Do you like it?' Pim's mother asked.

'Yes,' said Pim, 'it has a nice fresh smell.' He settled down by his mother for his feed. 'Mm-mm. So do you.'

'Yes, I probably do smell and taste a bit earthy,' laughed his mother. 'I'm glad you like it.'

Pim was soon full of warm milk. He stopped sucking, so his mouth was free to ask questions.

'Will I be able to dig a burrow like this?' he asked.

'Yes, dear. All aardvarks are good diggers, if they have enough sleep, that is. . . . '

Pim opened his mouth, but shut it again. He could take a hint.

He put snout to tail and went to sleep.

He woke up feeling very lively. He couldn't

31

wait to practise his digging. How could he be a proper aardvark until he could dig? He must start now. And there was a good place to begin – the shelter his mother had made the night before. There was one snag though. His mother was still fast asleep, so he couldn't ask her permission. Well, his plan was a safe one. He was sure she wouldn't mind. He crept past her and into the tunnel.

He was surprised to find that it was still light outside. In fact, it was only late afternoon, but that made no difference to his plan.

He sat on his tail and put up his ears and listened carefully. It seemed to be safe. He scampered over to the shallow burrow and went inside. Yes, the earth was still nice and soft. He stretched out his forefeet with their powerful claws and began to dig. Oh, this was easy.

But after a little while he began to realise that it was not as easy as all that. He soon found that he had a pile of earth under his tummy which got in the way. What did he do with it? The further forward he burrowed, the more earth he had piled up round him, under him and behind him. It had to go somewhere.

Then he remembered the shower of earth he'd had to dodge when he was watching his mother digging. She had kicked it out behind her with her hind legs. Pim began to kick.

But he had left it too late. His mother kicked it out behind her as she went along, so she never had more than a manageable amount to deal with at a time. Pim already had a small mountain behind him. He kicked harder and harder, but only succeeded in burying himself in it.

Poor Pim. He lay still, panting. Now what was he going to do? He had blocked the way out behind him. He would have to turn round and burrow his way out.

When he felt strong enough he would begin. . . . But what was that? There was something moving outside, just above him, something with a strong smell. He had never smelt it before but he knew what it was. Big cat smell – leopard or lion. It was the smell of danger.

Pim froze. He was only just under the ground. If the big cat heard him, it could probably reach him. Pim didn't want to end up as a tasty tea for a lion.

But now he was really stuck. He dare not burrow any deeper into the ground because he was such a rotten digger and anyway he might be heard. He couldn't go back to the surface and make a dive for his safe den with the big cat wandering about up there.

He was trapped. He would have to stay here until it was safe to come out.

Suddenly his ears pricked up and quivered. There were scraping sounds in the earth in front of him! Was the lion coming down for him that way? Pim was so frightened that he couldn't think any more. He just crouched there shivering with his eyes shut, while the sounds got nearer and nearer.

Something burst through the wall of earth in front of him. It was upon him!

'Pim?' his mother's voice whispered. 'I guessed you were here. Come on. I've made a tunnel.'

In a few moments Pim was safe in his burrow, cuddled close to his mother.

He told her all about what had happened and how he had thought she was a lion coming for him.

'Lions are rotten diggers,' his mother said. 'Anyway, what's this for?' She tweaked his trembling snout. 'If you had used this, you would have known it was me and not the lion. Well, never mind. It's all over now. Come and have your feed.'

Pim snuggled close to her and found a teat to suck. But before he took it in his mouth, he said, 'Are you sure I'm an aardvark?'

'Yes,' said his mother, 'quite sure.'

'Well, you said all aardvarks are good diggers. You were wrong. I'm a terrible digger.'

Mrs Aardvark smiled. 'Well, I should have said "except when they're very young". You

haven't been taught to dig yet. I'll give you a
lesson tomorrow.'

'And then I'll be a proper aardvark?'

'Pim, you *are* an aardvark. Nothing can
change that.'

But Pim wasn't absolutely sure.

5 · A long story

Pim was tired after his adventure, so his mother left him to sleep it off while she went out to find some termites. He was just waking up when she got back.

'Yes, I went without you,' she said, before he could start complaining, 'and it's a good job I did too. This is a dangerous place. We'll have to go back to our old burrow. We're very near a water-hole here.'

'Water's not dangerous,' said Pim. 'The elephants had a lot of fun in it.'

'Water is dangerous to us when it attracts so many animals. They come to drink there every evening, hundreds of them. It's the only drinking place for miles. That means there are lions going right past our front door.'

'Like yesterday!' said Pim. 'Like the one that frightened me yesterday.'

'That's right,' said his mother. 'We shall have to move again, which is a pity because there are lots of good termite nests in this area. Oh well, I must get some sleep.'

'I've *been* asleep,' Pim complained. 'I feel awake now. I couldn't sleep any more.'

'Well, you can go up to the top and sun yourself for a bit if you like, as you did the other morning, but stay very close to the burrow. In fact, keep your tail in the entrance tunnel.'

Pim bounded towards the tunnel and then stopped and came back. He had remembered something.

'Perhaps I won't go up after all. There might be lions.'

'Not at this time of the morning. They're lazy beasts.' Mrs Aardvark smiled. 'Not everything wants to eat you, you know.

38

You'll be all right if you do what you're told.'

Pim crept slowly up the tunnel. He peeped out and blinked. The sun had just risen and was already very bright. He pricked up his ears and listened carefully. Nothing. With most of him still inside the tunnel, Pim sat himself down. The sun was lovely and warm.

Sunbathing made him drowsy, and certainly his ears were not as pricked as they should have been or he might have heard his visitor coming. But it didn't bound, or hop or gallop. In fact it had no legs at all, so it just wriggled towards him through the grass very slowly.

The first thing Pim knew about it was when something tickled his ear. He put up a back foot and scratched the tickly place. He felt something there.

'You don't have to kick me,' said a voice.

'Sorry. I thought you were an itch,' Pim said. He looked at his visitor. He seemed

39

harmless enough – long and bendy like an elephant's trunk without the elephant. He had better make sure though.

'Do you want to eat me?' he asked, backing slowly into the burrow.

'Not particularly,' said the long, thin creature. 'You look a bit too big for me, and anyway I'm not hungry at the moment. Pythons don't eat very often.'

'Pythons? Is that what you are?' Pim stopped backing and took a good look at his visitor.

'Yes, I'm a python. What are you?'

'An aardvark.'

'An odd what?'

Pim was getting rather tired of people making this rude remark. 'An *aardvark*!'

'Oh, you look a bit piggy to me. Wait a minute. Aard-vark – earth-pig. That's what it means. You *are* a sort of pig.'

'Do pigs eat termites?' asked Pim. He wasn't a bit insulted about being called a pig – just interested. 'Aardvarks eat termites. At

40

least grown-up ones do. My mother eats them every night.'

'Oh?' The python had no idea what termites were, but he wasn't going to admit it. 'Your mother . . . do you see her often then? I only saw mine once. Just after I'd hatched. She. . . . Whoops! I think it's gone!'

'What's gone?' Pim stared at the little snake, who was searching the grass in front of him.

'My wiggly tooth. My egg tooth. Didn't you have one when you hatched? A special tooth for slitting the shell of your egg so that you could get out.'

'Er . . . I expect I did,' said Pim. 'I don't remember. Did you say you've only seen your mother once? Who feeds you then? Who looks after you?'

'I look after myself,' said the python. 'I don't expect I'll need feeding for months, and then I shall wrap myself round something and squash it and swallow it whole.' The little python couldn't resist teasing Pim a little.

'Something like you, I should think. You'd be very tasty.'

Pim backed hurriedly into the burrow. The python was only a little chap but. . . .

With a wicked glint in his eye, the python followed him a little way.

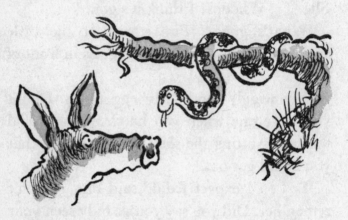

'May I practise on you?' he asked. 'It would be awfully helpful of you and I'd try not to squash you too much.'

Pim didn't feel like being awfully helpful. He turned and bolted down his hole. Mrs Aardvark opened one eye as her son scuttled in.

'Well, who wanted to eat you?' she asked.

'A python,' said Pim. His mother sat bolt upright. 'Oh, it was only a little one, but he said he thought I'd be tasty.'

'I daresay,' said Mrs Aardvark. 'You keep away from pythons. Big ones anyway.'

'This one had only just hatched,' said Pim. 'His egg tooth fell out while we were talking.'

'Oh, he *was* just a baby then.' Mrs Aardvark settled back in her sleeping position. Pim curled up too, but there was one more thing he wanted to ask.

'Was I hatched? I don't remember.'

'No. You were born.'

'What's born?'

'Well, you grew in my tummy and when you were ready to arrive, I landed you just as you are, not in an egg.'

Pim snuggled close to his mother. He thought about the poor little python who had to crack his way out of an egg by himself and had nobody to look after him or feed him or belong to.

'I'm glad I'm an aardvark,' Pim said. 'I'm glad I was born.'

6 · An ugly business

Late that evening, Pim and his mother crept out of their burrow and stood listening, ears and noses a-quiver. There had been a lot of traffic past their door earlier on – every animal in Africa seemed to be going to the water-hole – but now it was safe to come out.

'Come on,' Mrs Aardvark whispered. 'Keep close to me.'

Pim had every intention of keeping close to his mother. There were lots of strange smells about and he could hear odd bellows and roars in the distance. This was no place to linger by himself.

They galloped across the veldt towards

their old burrow. It wasn't really very far. Pim began to get excited when he recognised his old home ground.

'There's the baboons' look-out tree!' he shouted. 'We're there.'

He ran on ahead. 'I'll be first home,' he called over his shoulder.

But he had a shock when he bounded up to the burrow. Someone was there before him. An animal with an incredibly ugly face was blocking the entrance. It was standing there with great curving tusks pointing towards Pim! It looked very fierce indeed.

Pim backed away and ran to his mother. 'Mum! Keep away! There's a thing, a horrible thing. . . .'

'With tusks?' his mother asked. 'And an ugly face? Oh, it's just a warthog. I should have known that this might happen. The lazy things will always take over one of our burrows rather than dig a home for themselves. I expect it's a lady warthog who wants to have her babies there. We'll have to dig a new one, that's all.'

'You mean you're going to let her have it?' Pim said. 'Our burrow?'

'Do you feel like arguing with those tusks?' Mrs Aardvark said. 'I don't. Anyway you should be proud. It's because we are the best diggers in Africa that other animals want our dens.'

Pim thought about that as they moved on looking for a good place to make a burrow.

'Here we are,' his mother said at last. 'I like this place.' She looked around at the sandy soil in the sheltered spot she had chosen.

47

They were on a slight hill and would have a good view of the surrounding country.

'Mum,' Pim said. 'If we didn't dig such good burrows, other animals wouldn't want them, would they? We could keep them for ourselves. That would be much nicer.'

'Don't be silly, dear,' his mother said. 'Come on. I'll give you a digging lesson.'

'I'm not sure that I want to be a good digger,' Pim said stubbornly, sitting on his tail. 'If I make rotten burrows when I'm grown up, nobody will steal them, will they?'

'No, perhaps not. But the roof will probably fall in on you and you'll be buried alive. Or when you're caught far from your rotten burrow by an enemy, you won't be able to dig fast enough to get away from it. Either way, you won't last long. Please yourself. You needn't learn to dig if you don't want to.'

She turned away.

Pim decided that he did want to.

'All right,' he said. 'You can teach me to dig if you like. It might come in useful.'

So Pim had his digging lesson. He was taught how to sweep away with his back feet and his tail the earth he had dug up with his forefeet. He was also taught to fold down his ears. This was to keep the earth out of them.

'I wish I had known about this yesterday,' he said. 'It's very tickly, earth in the ears.'

'Yes,' his mother said. 'But you can pop them back up again now. It's time I made the burrow. Now watch.'

She began to dig at enormous speed. Earth and stones flew into the air behind her in a great shower.

She stopped and came up to see if Pim was all right.

He had his ears folded down and his eyes tight shut.

'What have you got your eyes shut for?' she said. 'How can you watch like that?'

'Because earth in the eyes is uncomfortable too,' he said. 'Have *you* ever tried to watch another aardvark digging? I'm all battered.'

49

'I'm sorry, dear,' Mrs Aardvark said. 'But you don't have to stand right in the line of fire, you know. Move over there a bit. That's right. I shan't be long.'

She dived in again and there was a new burrow waiting in no time at all. Mrs Aardvark came up to invite Pim to come and inspect it.

'Well?' she said. 'Will it do?'

'It will do,' said Pim looking round at the neat chamber under the ground. 'If I were a warthog, I just couldn't wait to come and pinch it.'

'Pim!' Mrs Aardvark said warningly. 'Go

and build yourself a rotten den then. Go on, cleversticks!'

'I will,' Pim said. 'When I can dig as well as you I will, but this will do for now.' He grinned at his mother. 'When I'm grown up I'll build a burrow that every animal in Africa will want for his own, not just a few ugly old warthogs. All the animals will know that I'm the best digger in the world. Can I have my feed now?'

'Yes,' his mother said, settling down on the earth floor. 'You may. So you've decided to be a good digger after all, have you?'

'Yes,' said Pim with his mouth full. Then he leaned back and looked up at his mother. 'Well, I can't help it, can I? I'm an aardvark.'

7 · A tall story

Mrs Aardvark spent the rest of the night hunting for termite hills. Pim didn't go with her as he was tired after his digging lesson. He went to sleep in the new burrow and, of course, he was just waking up as his mother came home at dawn to sleep.

'All right,' she said when she saw his hopeful face, 'after your feed you can go up top for a while. Don't be too long though: I'm ready for a good day's sleep.'

Soon Pim was scampering up the tunnel. He popped his head out and listened. Nothing.

He ventured out a little further when his night eyes had become used to the light. This *was* an interesting place. The new burrow was on a sort of shelf. There were what looked like the tops of trees scalloping the edge of it, and beyond them the veldt stretched out as far as he could see.

Suddenly he heard something. There was a sort of munching noise coming from the tree-tops. Monkeys?

Very cautiously, his tail leaving a trail in the sand, Pim moved towards the sound. As he neared the edge of the shelf, which was really a small cliff, Pim saw that the sound was being made by a long, pink tongue plucking leaves from a tree.

The owner of the tongue saw Pim at the same time as Pim saw her. Shyly she jerked back her head which was balanced on a long, long neck that seemed to go down for ever. Pim couldn't help staring. He peeped over the edge of the cliff. She went right down to the ground below! She had not climbed up the tree as he had at first thought. She was as tall as the tree!

Pim forgot about being polite.

'What *are* you?' he said, goggling.

'Me? I'm just a giraffe.' She smiled at Pim in a friendly way. 'Haven't you seen a giraffe before?'

'No, I haven't,' Pim said. 'You . . . you're very tall, aren't you?'

'I suppose I am. I have to be to reach my food. I've never seen anyone like you either. What are you?'

'An aardvark.' Pim waited for the usual reply.

'An odd . . . ? I'm sorry, I didn't quite catch it.'

Well, this was a change at any rate. Mind you, Miss Giraffe was in no position to find anyone else an oddity.

'An *aardvark*,' Pim said clearly. 'I live under the ground, and you live a long way above it.'

'Well yes,' Miss Giraffe admitted. 'I find reaching down to the ground rather difficult, actually. Drinking is terribly difficult. My legs are so long and my knees won't bend properly. I have to straddle them out sideways and bend my head down in between them to the water. It's a good job I have a long neck.'

'Show me,' Pim said.

Miss Giraffe showed him, which was very kind of her, seeing that it was such an uncomfortable position for her.

'Yes, I see what you mean,' Pim said when her head came up again. 'How do you get down to sleep? It must be very difficult.'

'I don't,' Miss Giraffe said. 'I sleep standing up.'

'Oh,' Pim said. 'Do you know, I probably would never have met you at all if I hadn't been up here on this cliff. Not to talk to.'

'Now, you show me something,' Miss Giraffe said.

That foxed him. 'What sort of something?' he asked.

'Well, something special that you can do because you're an aardvark.'

Pim thought hard. 'Well, I can dig,' he said. 'Can you dig?'

'No,' said Miss Giraffe. 'Show me.'

So Pim, delighted to show off, dug a hole very fast, shooting earth into the air behind him with his hind legs and tail.

Miss Giraffe was very impressed.

'But why are your ears all flat like that?' she said when he popped his head out of the hole again. 'You do look funny.'

'Keeps the earth out,' Pim said. He had thought of something else he could do. 'I can stick my tongue in and out very fast,' he said. 'Watch!'

'I can do that too,' Miss Giraffe said. 'There. My tongue is just as long as yours.'

And so began a tongue-sticking-out match. That is how poor sleepy Mrs Aardvark found them when she came out to see why Pim had been such a long time.

'Really, Pim,' she said. 'You are very rude! I apologise for my son's manners, Miss Giraffe. He should know better.'

'Oh, that's all right, Mrs Aardvark,' Miss Giraffe said, winking at Pim. 'I asked him to.

But I must go now. My mother will be looking for me. Goodbye.' She turned and galloped away, her head and neck swaying forwards and backwards in a steady rhythm.

Pim watched her go quite sadly.

'She was nice,' he told his mother, 'but I'm glad I don't have to sleep standing up.'

'I shall be grateful to get any sleep at all

today,' Mrs Aardvark snapped, 'even if I have to stand on my head.'

Pim decided that it would be unwise to keep her from the burrow any longer.

8 · A fast one

Mrs Aardvark got her sleep. She and Pim slept all day and then they were ready at nightfall for their termite hunt.

They came out of the tunnel into bright moonlight. It was almost as light as day.

'We'll have to be very careful tonight,' Mrs Aardvark said as they moved off. 'There'll be a lot of predators about.'

'Predators?' said Pim. 'What are they?'

'Well, they're animals that may fancy an aardvark for supper,' Mrs Aardvark said. 'Lions and leopards and cheetahs. . . .'

'I haven't heard of them. What's a cheetah?'

'Oh, another sort of big cat. They're very fast runners. Faster than anything I have ever seen.'

Pim looked down at his clumsy feet lolloping along. 'How do we get away from them then?'

'The usual way. Find a hole to shelter in or dig one quickly. If we're really cornered, we can always fight, of course. I had to fight a cheetah once.'

'Did you win?' asked Pim, gazing at his mother wide-eyed.

'I did,' she said grimly. 'I wouldn't be here otherwise. But I was lucky. It's best to get away from them by digging if you can.'

Pim looked about him fearfully. He did not fancy his chances of digging faster than a cheetah could run, even if he saw one coming a long way away.

'I think you'd better teach me how to fight. Soon!' he said.

'All right,' his mother said. 'I suppose it's about time you learned, although if you didn't keep wandering off by yourself it wouldn't be necessary. I'm here to defend you – that's what mothers are for.'

'Oh good,' Pim said, moving very close to her. 'If a cheetah chases us, will you dig us a hole or fight it?' He was rather looking forward to watching a good fight.

'Wait and see,' said his mother. 'It may never happen.'

It didn't. They reached a patch of termite hills without even smelling 'big cat', never mind hearing any distant roars. Pim was almost disappointed.

'Now, don't go wandering off,' said his mother as she set about breaching a tall termite nest. 'You stay near me.'

Pim looked around him. There were some very interesting looking bushes by a funny shaped tree just across the clearing.

'Can I go over there?' he asked. 'I'll be very good and not go any further.'

His mother broke off her attack on the nest and looked at the bushes.

'All right,' she said. 'But come back at once if you hear or smell anything dangerous.'

Pim scampered over to the bushes. There was nothing there.

Not at first, that is. He had only been there a few minutes when a tangled ball of young animals came rolling past him – he was hid-

den from them by a bush – making squeaking noises. They were obviously fighting each other, or rather playing at fighting each other.

One of them broke away from the others and climbed on to a low branch of the tree. Pim could see him more clearly. It looked as if he had been crying black tears – he had two dark lines from his eyes down to his mouth. He was covered with spots. The fur on his back was long and fluffy but underneath he was smooth and dark. He was balancing on the branch with the help of a long, spotted tail.

Suddenly he sprang down, tumbling his brothers and sisters in all directions. They turned on him with little growls and squeaks. The fighting got quite fierce.

Pim was dying to join in; they were having such fun.

There was just one thing bothering him, though. They were quite small and didn't look a bit dangerous, but they smelled . . . well, catty. He was an aardvark after all and 'cat' meant danger.

But now they didn't look a bit dangerous. They had stopped scuffling and were all cuddled together. One of them was licking the smallest one; perhaps he had come off worst in the fight. The others were making a nice soft purring sound. A very peaceful and contented sound it seemed to Pim. Surely they couldn't be cats!

He had to find out. Pim came out from behind his bush and walked towards them.

When they saw him they jumped up and huddled together. The biggest one said, 'What are you?'

'An aardvark,' Pim said. 'I was just wondering . . . .'

'An odd what?' the spotted animal said, and the others tittered.

'An *aardvark*,' Pim said. 'I eat termites.'

'Oh, we're cheetahs,' the cub said, 'and we eat aardvarks!'

'Not this one, you don't,' said Pim, turning and bolting back to his mother.

The cheetah cubs pretended to chase him but there were tired after their fight and, of course, they were much too young to eat aardvarks.

When she saw Pim running towards her, Mrs Aardvark quickly swallowed her last termite.

'Cheetahs!' gasped Pim.

'In here then!' said his mother, and shoved

him inside the empty termite nest. With great speed she dug herself deep into the ground.

Just in time. The cubs' mother came back and smelled aardvark. But she soon lost interest when she couldn't find them and, anyway, she had a hungry family to feed.

When she had gone, Mrs Aardvark collected Pim and they galloped home across the veldt.

'How did you know that cheetah was coming?' Mrs Aardvark asked Pim.

'Er . . . because I'm an aardvark,' he said loftily. 'I smelled it.'

His mother was not impressed.

'Rubbish,' she said, 'that's a whopper. Now tell me the truth.'

So Pim told her all about it.

9 · A spiky one

Next evening Mrs Aardvark gave Pim a fighting lesson outside the burrow.

'Mind you, I don't think I really need to tell you what to do,' Pim's mother said as they went up the tunnel. 'Instinct will tell you.'

'Who's instinct?' Pim said.

'*What's* instinct,' Mrs Aardvark said. 'Well, it's the voice inside you that tells you important things you need to know. Remember when the lion came sniffing about when you were trapped under the ground? You couldn't see it, but I expect you could smell it. Well, how did you know that it was a big cat?'

'I just knew,' Pim said.

'Yes. Well, that was instinct working. Now, let's see if it will work for you again. I'm going to be a cheetah.'

'A lion,' Pim said.

'All right, I'm a lion. Now you stand over there under that tree. I'll pounce on you suddenly. I think you'll know what to do.'

'Will you roar?' Pim thought this was a good game.

'No, I can't. You'll have to imagine that bit. Now, I'm a lion, remember.'

Pim stood in front of the tree and waited. His mother *was* a long time. He looked up. This was a funny tree with a long thin trunk and the top spreading out like an umbrella. There was something moving up there. Was it a bird or a squirrel? Pim peered a bit harder.

Mrs Aardvark pounced.

At once Pim rolled over on to his back and began lashing at her with all four feet, his claws fully out. He even struck at her with his tail.

'All right!' Mrs Aardvark gasped, trying to hold him off. 'I'm just your mother. Stop.'

Pim sat up slowly.

'You said you were a lion,' he grumbled. 'I wish you'd make up your mind.'

His mother looked at him.

'I'm glad I'm not a lion,' she said, 'if that's how you treat them.'

Pim suddenly realized. 'I *knew*!' he shouted. 'I knew how to fight!'

'You knew all right,' said his mother, feeling the tender spots all over her. 'It's a good job I have a very thick hide. If I'd had a thin skin like a cat I would have been scratched and ripped and torn. Ugh!'

Pim was very pleased with himself.

'Isn't instinct wonderful?' he cried. 'Shall we have another fight tomorrow?'

'No, thank you,' Mrs Aardvark said. 'That's your last fighting lesson.'

'But it's only my first fighting lesson,' said Pim.

'It's the first and the last,' his mother said firmly. She felt very sore. 'Come on. If we're to find some termite nests before dawn, we must get going.'

And so that night and the next one and every night for the next five months, Pim accompanied his mother on her hunting trips. He also grew bigger and stronger.

He practised digging a lot and became quite expert. They moved house several times and each time Pim helped his mother dig the new burrow.

But one night Mrs Aardvark said, 'I don't want you to help me this time.'

'Why not?' said Pim. 'I know what to do.'

'Yes, you do. So you can make yourself a burrow, can't you?'

Pim beamed at her. 'Yes! Yes, I will.'

So Pim dug his first burrow. He made a long tunnel and then dug out a round chamber at the end of it big enough to turn round in.

Proudly he brought his mother down to inspect it.

'Yes, it's good,' she said, looking round her. 'I thought you said you were going to build rotten burrows that warthogs wouldn't want.'

'If any warthog tries to pinch this, he will have me to reckon with,' Pim said fiercely.

It wasn't a warthog, it was a porcupine. Pim met him coming down the tunnel the next evening. The porcupine backed hastily in front of Pim.

'I'm s-sorry. I didn't know anybody lived here,' he said. 'I-I didn't mean to intrude. Really I didn't.' His quills rattled nervously.

'What made you think you could just walk in here when you felt like it?' Pim said fiercely. 'You've got a cheek!'

'Oh d-dear,' said the little porcupine. 'My mother t-t-told me that empty aardvark b-burrows make the b-b-best homes, you see.'

'This aardvark burrow isn't empty,' Pim said.

'No, I-I can see that,' said the little porcupine, his quills rattling more than ever. 'I-I'll g-go at once.' He turned and began to rattle away with a sharp shuffling gait.

'Wait!' Pim said. 'I forgive you. Please come back, little . . . what are you?'

'A porcupine.' The creature came back slowly.

'What can you do?' Pim asked. 'I'm just interested.'

'D-do?' the porcupine said. 'Well, I can climb trees and swim.'

'Swim?'

'Yes, you know, m-move in the water to cross rivers and p-pools. Can you swim?'

'Er . . . of course,' said Pim. 'What else can you do? Can you fight?'

'Of course,' said the little porcupine. 'I make my quills stand up like this, and then I rush at my attacker – like this.' He charged at Pim, but stopped just short of him.

Pim was very relieved. It would have been very painful indeed to have all those sharp quills stuck into him at once.

'Yes, I see,' he said. 'Er . . . what do you eat?'

'Oh, grass and bark and things like that. What do you eat?'

'Termites,' Pim said. 'I was just going to hunt for some as a matter of fact.'

'Oh, well I won't keep you then. Goodbye. Thank you for being so nice.' The porcupine shuffled off.

He happened to look round a second or two later, in time to see the friendly aardvark turning into another burrow. That was a funny place to look for termites. Oh well, it was nothing to do with him. The porcupine continued on his way.

He wasn't to know that Pim wasn't weaned yet; that he was heading for his mother and some milk.

10 · The last one

Pim went out with his mother after his feed as usual.

Mrs Aardvark had a problem. Pim was six months old now, which is quite grown up for an aardvark, and it was time he began to eat termites.

But Pim wasn't interested in termites. She had taught him to tear open their nests. She had taught him to close his nostrils to keep the insects out while he was working. She had taught him how to use his tongue. But she couldn't teach him to want to eat termites, and while he was full of milk, hunger wouldn't drive him to try them.

There was only one thing to do, and when they got back to her burrow Mrs Aardvark did it.

'Good night, Pim,' she said, as she stopped at the entrance to her burrow.

'Good night already?' Pim said. 'What about my feed?'

'Oh, you're too grown up for milk now. I'm not going to feed you any more. Good night, dear.'

She turned her back and disappeared down her entrance tunnel. She felt terribly mean but it was the only way.

Pim went down his entrance tunnel feeling very cross indeed. How could his mother refuse to feed him just like that? What a cruel thing to do. He felt very hard-done-by and muttered to himself as he dropped off to sleep.

77

His mother hardly slept at all. She lay there worrying about him all day.

When Pim woke up that evening he was hungry, but he couldn't bring himself to go to his mother's burrow and be refused again. He lay there sulking and wondering what to do.

Suddenly he heard something, something he had never heard before. It sounded like

thousands of tiny feet marching! It couldn't be. He listened very carefully. There was no doubt about it – tiny footfalls – that's what he could hear. Pim dashed up the tunnel to see what it could be. His ears must be playing tricks.

They weren't. Not far from the burrow there was a long wavy line of termites marching. Pim knew what they were by the smell, even before he was near enough to see what they were. Termites on the march, thousands of them!

And for the first time Pim saw them as they really were – *food*! Food marching right past his front door! He wouldn't even have to go searching for it. Food that he didn't have to dig for.

It was just too easy. All he had to do was put out his long sticky tongue. . . .

M-m-m-m! They were really very good. He shot out his tongue again and again. Soon he was gobbling termites as fast as he could go.

Mrs Aardvark had also heard the termites and come up, but when she saw Pim she stayed where she was. At last! She needn't worry about him any more. He liked termites.

Pim *did* like termites, and there wasn't much left of that wavy line of them by the time he had eaten his fill.

As he went back towards his burrow he saw his mother watching him.

'It's all right,' he said. 'I'm a grown-up

aardvark now. I shan't need you any more.' Suddenly he galloped over to her. 'If you hurry up you can still catch some termites. I didn't eat them all.'

'Oh good,' said Mrs Aardvark. 'Thank you, my son.' She galloped happily away to chase the tail of the termite column. Her job was done.

Pim crawled into his burrow. He settled down in his sleeping corner, tired and happy and full. Oh, termites *were* delicious. To-morrow night he would go out hunting and find some more – lots more.

Pim looked around him at the firm earth walls of his home. Yes, this was a good burrow – and he had made it all himself.

He sighed happily and buried his snout in his tail.

There was no doubt about it now.

Pim was an aardvark.